Especially for baby Edith, with love
~ M. C. B.

For Harriet James
~ T. M.

tiger tales
5 River Road, Suite 128, Wilton, CT 06897
Published in the United States 2019
Originally published in Great Britain 2019
by Little Tiger Press Ltd.
Text copyright © 2019 M. Christina Butler
Illustrations copyright © 2019 Tina Macnaughton
ISBN-13: 978-1-68010-155-3
ISBN-10: 1-68010-155-2
Printed in China
LTP/1800/2648/0219

For more insight and activities, visit us at www.tigertalesbooks.com

One Christmas Adventure

by M. Christina Butler • Illustrated by Tina Macnaughton

tiger tales

Little Hedgehog and his friends were out walking in the snow, gathering holly for their Christmas party.

"What's that?" exclaimed Fox as a strange figure wobbled toward them.

"Is it a present on legs?" cried Rabbit.

"No," chuckled Little Hedgehog. "I think it's Squirrel!"

"Where are you going with all of those things?" asked Little Hedgehog, rushing up to help.

"Hello," gasped Squirrel. "I'm taking Christmas presents and snacks to Grandpa Squirrel. He has a terrible cold and can't get out in all this snow."

"We'll help you!" offered Little Hedgehog.
"Come on, everyone!"
"Oh, thank you!" beamed Squirrel.

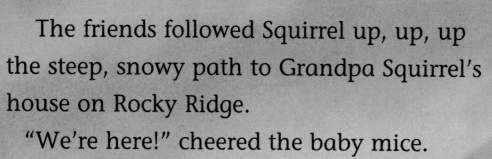

The friends followed Squirrel up, up, up
the steep, snowy path to Grandpa Squirrel's
house on Rocky Ridge.

"We're here!" cheered the baby mice.

"Oh, my!" declared Grandpa Squirrel, opening
his door. "Come in! What a wonderful surprise!
I'll make some hot chocolate to warm you up."

As they shared stories and nibbled cookies, Little Hedgehog noticed fresh flakes of snow falling outside.

"We'd better get going," he said.

"Thanks for all your help!" exclaimed Squirrel.

"Be careful," warned Grandpa Squirrel. "The path can get very slippery."

In a flurry of snowflakes
the friends slowly made their
way down the icy path.
"Careful, everyone!" cried
Badger.
But it was too late . . . .

Whoosh!

Little Hedgehog slipped.

"Look out!" he called.

But then Fox skidded into Badger, who bumped into Rabbit and all the mice! Soon everyone was slip-sliding down the path.

Thud! They landed in a snowy heap.

"Is everyone all right?"
gasped Little Hedgehog.

"We're fine!" squeaked Mouse.

"So are we!" added Fox and Badger.
"That just leaves . . ."

"Rabbit!" they all called. "Where
are you, Rabbit?"

And their cries echoed
around the mountain.

"Here I am!" answered Rabbit from under a snowy drift. "But what's that rumbling sound?"

They looked at each other as the snow began to shudder and shake.

"AVALANCHE!" yelled Badger. "Quick! Everyone into this cave!"

Swoosh!

Safely inside, the friends peered out as
a rush of snow swept past the cave.
"That was close!" said Fox. All at once
the snow stopped, and everything was still.

"The snow is covering the path!" squeaked
Mouse as they stepped outside.

"We're stuck!" cried Rabbit. "We'll miss
Christmas!"

"There must be another way home," said
Badger. "I think we can climb down the
side of the mountain."

"But it'll be dark soon,"
shivered a baby mouse.
"We might get lost!"

"I know what to do!" said
Little Hedgehog, unraveling
his hat. "We'll use this yarn
to tie ourselves together.
That way, we won't get
separated as we climb
down!"

Little Hedgehog tied one end
of the yarn to a tree. Then everyone
wrapped the yarn around their waists.
"Take your time, and be careful!"
warned Badger as they began to
make their way down the mountain.

"We're almost there!" called Little Hedgehog,
leading the way. But the yarn was wet
and slippery between his paws.
"Oh, no!" he cried, starting to slide.
"The yarn is running out!"
Down,

down,

down, he slipped . . .

. . . until the bright red
pom-pom stopped his fall!
"I'm okay!" he shouted.
"I've been saved by
my hat!"
"Hooray!" everyone
cheered, jumping safely
to the ground.

"What an adventure!" said Little Hedgehog
as the friends walked up to Badger's house.
"But look at my poor hat . . . ."
"Don't worry," smiled Badger kindly.
"We can fix that!"

And that's just what they did!

With cupcakes and mugs of hot chocolate, Badger showed Little Hedgehog how to knit his hat back together.

"My favorite hat will be as good as new!" smiled Little Hedgehog. "Thank you, Badger! And Merry Christmas, everyone!"